MY BOOK

First Parish in Bedford
75 The Great Road
Bedford, MA 01730
781-275-7994

THE
Flyaway Kite

GYO FUJIKAWA

GROSSET & DUNLAP · PUBLISHERS · NEW YORK

A FILMWAYS COMPANY

Library of Congress Catalog Card Number: 80-83353. ISBN: 0-448-11747-9 (Trade Edition): ISBN: 0-448-13652-X (Library Edition).

Nicholas wanted to borrow Sam's brand-new kite.

"Can I fly your kite, Sam?" Nicholas asked.
"I'll be careful."

"O.K. I have to go home for lunch now. You can
fly it until I get back," Sam said.

Nicholas took hold of the
kite string and ran off.

"Come on, kite," Nicholas said.
"I'll race you."

The faster Nicholas ran,
the better the kite flew.
It followed him with its slinky,
shaky tail waving every which
way in the breeze.

Suddenly,
Nicholas stumbled and fell —
   and the kite string slid right out of his hand.

The kite flew up and up and up, higher and higher.
"Come back!" Nicholas yelled.
But the kite flew even faster — and then
it was over the treetops and out of sight.
Nicholas didn't know what to do.
What would he tell Sam? Just then,
he heard his friend Jenny calling:
"Nicholas! Sam told me you had his
new kite. I want to fly it, too."

"You can't fly it, Jenny," Nicholas said,
"because . . . a great big elephant stepped
on it and broke it all to pieces."

"An elephant!" Jenny said.
"Where did it come from?"

"There was a circus parade
in the woods," Nicholas said,
"with lions and tigers and acrobats
and clowns and elephants and
everything."

"A circus parade!" Jenny said.
"I want to see it!"

And off she rushed.

Nicholas wondered if Sam would believe
the elephant story. Before he could make up
his mind, he saw Mei Su coming.

"Sam said for you to let me fly his kite,"
Mei Su said. "Where is it?"

"It's gone, Mei Su," Nicholas told his friend.
"A giant eagle was up there in the sky.

"All of a sudden, it swooped
down and grabbed the kite
and flew away with it."

"An eagle!" Mei Su said.
"Oh, that's terrible!
    It might try to get us!"

Jenny came running back.
"I didn't see any circus parade,
Nicholas," Jenny said. "And I didn't
see the elephant that stepped on
Sam's kite and broke it."

"But, Nicholas," Mei Su
said. "You told me an eagle
flew away with Sam's kite."

"Well," Nicholas said. "It wasn't an elephant, and it wasn't an eagle. It was an awful dragon. Fire came out of its nose and . . ."

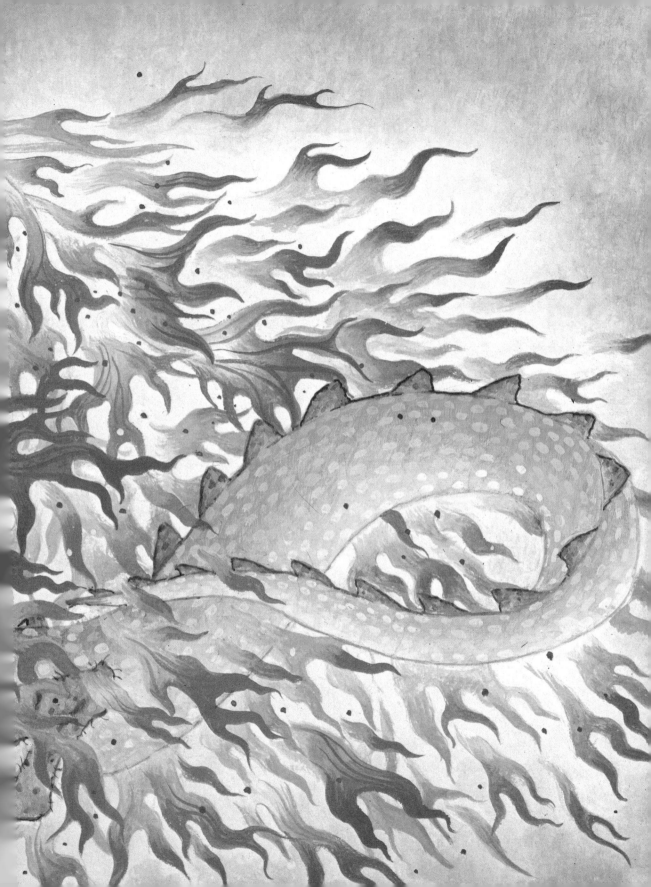

Just then, Nicholas saw Sam and Shags coming.
He stopped talking and ran behind a tree.
"Don't tell Sam you've seen me," Nicholas said.
"Why not?" Jenny asked.
"Because . . . I lost his kite," Nicholas said.
"I fell down and let go of the string.
And the kite flew away."
"It wasn't an elephant who stepped on it," Jenny said.
"Or a bad old eagle who took it. Or a dragon," Mei Su said.

Nicholas shook his head.
"No, I did it. I guess I'd better tell him."
So Nicholas told Sam what had really happened.
"I'm sorry, Sam. But I've got some money in
my piggy bank. I'll get you a new kite."

"The kite's not lost," Sam said. "I found it.
The string was caught in a tree near my house.
I need help to get it down. Come on."

The four friends ran to where the kite was caught in the tree. And soon they got it free.

Sam was happy because he had his kite back.

Jenny and Mei Su were happy because now they could fly the kite.

But Nicholas was the happiest of them all.
Everything had turned out all right.